# PARABLES

# PARABLES

Parables For Christ, To Reveal
The Mystery Of The Kingdom Of God In This Life

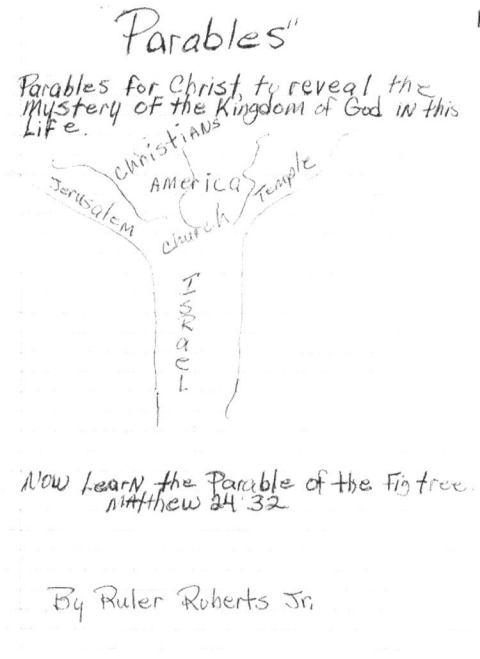

*Now Learn The Parable Of The Fig Tree*
MATTHEW 24:32

# RULER ROBERTS JR.

ReadersMagnet, LLC

*Parables*
Copyright © 2021 by Ruler Roberts Jr.

Published in the United States of America
ISBN Paperback: 978-1-956780-75-8
ISBN eBook: 978-1-956780-74-1

All rights reserved. No part of this publication may be reproduced, stored in a retrieval system or transmitted in any way by any means, electronic, mechanical, photocopy, recording or otherwise without the prior permission of the author except as provided by USA copyright law.

The opinions expressed by the author are not necessarily those of ReadersMagnet, LLC.

ReadersMagnet, LLC
10620 Treena Street, Suite 230 | San Diego, California, 92131 USA
1.619. 354. 2643 | www.readersmagnet.com

Book design copyright © 2021 by ReadersMagnet, LLC. All rights reserved.
*Cover design by Ericka Obando*
*Interior design by Mary Mae Romero*

# INTRODUCTION

# PARABLES

Finally, the mystery of the Kingdom of God which is to come in apocalyptic power as foreseen by Prophet Daniel has entered the world in advance as parables in hidden form to work secretly within and among men. "Remember the former things of old: for I am God, and there is none like me." "Declaring the end form the beginning and from ancient times the things that are not yet done saying my counsel shall stand, and I will do all my pleasure. Isaiah 46: 9-10.

God is telling us to pay attention to the ancient times because he declared the end, in the beginning and it shall come to pass. How does he do these things? They are done in parables!

Jesus said in Mark 4:11 "and he said unto them, unto you it is given to know the mystery of the Kingdom of God. But unto them that are without, all these things are done in parables.

Parables are not just a story that Jesus use in the New Testament during his teaching of the gospel. But can be a person, place or thing in a real life event or action that was ordain by God before the ages for our glory. Parables are illustration of either good or evil, righteousness or wickedness to serve God purpose, from Genesis to Revelation, God revealed the knowledge of mysteries of the kingdom in this life through Parables.

# CHAPTER 1

# THE PURPOSE OF PARABLES

Parables serve as an example. The Parables by Jesus is a sample earthly story used to exemplify a moral or spiritual lesson of the kingdom as told by Jesus in the gospels in the New Testament, also in the Old Testament to reveal God's kingdom in the form of prophetic acts and events.

Parables are used in giving one or more instructional lesson or principles and can be an allegory and may include inanimate objects like trees, plants or things and people in various societal positions.

There is often a tension between good and evil or sinful and holy, meaning that they can proclaim what is good or bad, what is holy and God like or what is evil like Satan. A parable is often a significant comparison between 2 objects to teach a single concept or lesson. Some parables exemplify the principles, qualities and defining characteristics of Jesus in this life in the earth, and some are Anti-Christ.

In Mark Chapter 4, Jesus teaches how parables are heard and received by his disciples not by those who reject him.

In the sower and the seed, the seed is the word and the soil is the heart of man. Remember, the seed is the word of God, not money in this scripture.

## St. Mark Chapter 4

| | |
|---|---|
| Verse 1: | And he began again to teach by the sea side and there was gathered unto him a great multitude, so that he entered into a ship, and sat in the sea and the whole multitude was by the sea on the land. |
| Verse 2: | And he taught them many things by parables and said unto them in his doctrine. |
| Verse 3: | Behold, there went out a sower to sow. |
| Verse 4: | And it came to pass as he sowed some fell by the way side and the fowls of the air came and devoured it up. |
| Verse 5: | And some fell on stony ground, where it had not much earth and immediately it sprang up, because it had no depth of earth. |
| Verse 6: | But when the sun was up, it was scorched; and because it had no root, it withered away. |
| Verse 7: | And some fell among thorns, and the thorns grew up and choked it and it yielded no fruit. |
| Verse 8: | And other fell on good ground and did yield fruit that sprang up and increased and brought forth, some thirty and some sixty and some an hundred. |
| Verse 9: | And he said unto them, He that hath ears to hear, let him hear. |
| Verse 10: | And when he was alone, they that were about him with the twelve asked of him the parable. |

Verse:      11 is the scripture which confirmed the revelation that was given to me.

Verse 11:   And he said unto them, unto you it is given to know the mystery of the kingdom of God: but unto them that are without, all *these* things are done in parables.

Verse 12:   That seeing they may see, and not perceive; and hearing they may hear, and not understand; lest at any time they should be converted, and *their* sins should be forgiven them.

Verse 13:   And he said unto them, know ye not this parable? And how then will ye know all parables?

Verse 14:   The sower soweth the word.

Verse 15:   And these are they by the way side, where the word is sown; but when they have heard, Satan cometh immediately, and taketh away the word that was sown in their hearts.

Verse 16:   And these are they likewise which are sown on stony ground; who, when they have heard the word, immediately receive it with gladness.

Verse 17:   And have no root in themselves, and so endure but for a time: afterward, when affliction or persecution ariseth for the word's sake, immediately they are offended.

Verse 18:   And these are they which are sown among thorns; such as hear the word.

Verse 19:   And the cares of this world, and the deceitfulness of riches, and the lusts of other things entering in, choke the word, and it becometh unfruitful.

Verse 20:   And these are they which are sown on good ground; such as hear the word, and receive it, and bring forth fruit, some thirtyfold, some sixty, and some an hundred.

Verse 21:   And he said unto them, Is a candle brought to be put under a bushel, or under a bed? and not to be set on a candlestick?

Verse 22:   For there is nothing hid, which shall not be manifested; neither was anything kept secret, but that it should come abroad.

Verse 23:   If any man have ears to hear, let him hear.

Verse 24:   And he said unto them, Take heed what ye hear: with what measure ye mete, it shall be measured to you: and unto you that hear shall more be given.

Verse 25:   For he that hath, to him shall be given: and he that hath not, from him shall be taken even that which he hath.

These verses are about the soil which is the heart.

Verse 30:   And he said, whereunto shall we liken the kingdom of God? or with that comparison shall we compare it?

Verse 31:   It is like a grain of mustard seed, which, when it is sown in the earth, is less than all the seeds that be in the earth:

Verse 32:   But when it is sown, it growth up, and becometh greater than all herbs, and shooteth out great branches; so that the fowls of the air may lodge under the shadow of it.

Verse 33: And with many such parables spake he the word unto them, as they were able to hear it.
Verse 34: But without a parable spake he not unto them: and when they were alone, he expounded all things to his disciples.

Think about that for a moment, verse 34. He only spake by parables so we know that Jesus is the same yesterday, today and forevermore.

A. Malachi 3: Verse 6 "I am the Lord thy God I change not, therefore will he not only speak by parables today? So when God says in Isaiah 46:10 that he declared the end in the beginning and from ancient time it was done by his parables. Here are some examples: Father Abraham offering his son Isaac for a burnt offering. (Gen, 22:2)
God the Father would give his only begotten son as a sacrificial lamb.

B. Mathew 24:3-39. But as the days of Noah were so shall also the coming of the son of man be. For as in the days that were before the flood they were eating and drinking, marrying and giving in marriage, until the day that Noah entered into the ark and knew not until the flood came and took them away: so shall also the coming of the son of man be. Here Matthew is comparing the end times to the ancient times of Noah in the beginning.

C. In numbers 24 verse 3, God call Balaam directly a parable. "And he took up his parable and said, Balaam the son of Beor has said, and the man whose eyes are open hath said. I will reveal whom Balaam parable is in a another chapter.

D. And in Exodus 12 verse 7, "and they shall take of the blood and strike it on the two side posts and on the upper door post of the houses, wherein they shall eat it. This is an earthly story (parable) of our Lord and savior Jesus Christ blood stain cross.

The blood stain cross (Crucifixion of Christ) was a mystery. That's why Paul wrote in Corinthians 2:7-8, "But we speak the wisdom of God in a mystery, the hidden wisdom which God ordained before the ages for our glory, which none of the rulers of this age knew for had they known they would not have crucified the Lord of Glory.

Paul has made it clear that God's plan to bring salvation to those believe in Christ's death for their sin can only be known through the Holy Spirit. Human reason and senses are not enough. At best, that can lead to knowledge about God but not trusting faith in God. The Holy Spirit must reveal God's thoughts to us.

Not every believer will be able to interpret and fully understand these spiritual truths. That's why the apostles work as interpreters, helping those who have accepted Christ and heard from God through the holy spirit to better understand what it mean. A key aspect of discipleship, that's more gifted, mature and experienced Christians guide new believers on their growth.

The apostle knows they are not the one who makes it possible for anyone to believe. God must reveal the truth through his spirit to each person who will believe. Their job is simply to use words to help those who believe or who will believe to understand what cannot be known with human wisdom alone, in other words speaking words given to us by the spirit, using the spirits words to explain spiritual truths.

Therefore, in the history of man every event or situation has a spiritual reality. What you are seeing in the natural is the fruit of a seed, obedience or disobedience to the spirit of life-God. From Genesis to Revelation, God reveal the law of sowing and reaping when he created the natural world and everything to reproduce after its own kind. When he formed Adam, he breathed life into Adam from his on substance and nature. His design was perfect and his pleasure in mankind was complete. However, before the first natural conception, their act of disobedience sowed a spiritual seed of sin and death into their lives and bodies. That seed produced a deadly harvest of which you and I are a part of. Their offspring have been born after their own kind with a terminal disease of sin and death. Adam and Eve had a breakdown or disconnect or defect in their relationship with God. They were no longer spiritually connected. That is why we must be born again of the spirit of God to receive from God. Not just his promises and blessing, but his knowledge of the mysteries of the kingdom of God.

Paul explain the spiritual reality of warfare in Ephesians 6:10-20

10. Finally, my brethren, be strong in the Lord, and in the power of his might.
11. Put on the whole armour of God, that ye may be able to stand against the wiles of the devil.
12. For we do not wrestle not against powers, against the rulers of the darkness of this world, against spiritual wickedness in high places.
13. Wherefore take unto the whole armour of God, that ye may be able to withstand in the eveil day, and having done all, to stand.
14. Stand therefore, having your loins girt about with truth, and having on the breastplate of righteousness;
15. And your feet shod with the preparation of the gospel of peace;
16. Above all, taking the shield of faith, wherewith ye shall be able to quench all the fiery darts of the wicked.

17. And take the helmet of salvation, and the sword of the Spirit, which is the word of God:
18. Praying always with all prayer and supplication in the Spirit, and watching thereunto with all perseverance and supplication for all saints;
19. And for me, that utterance may be given unto me, that I may open my mouth boldly, to make known the mystery of the gospel.
20. For which I am an ambassador in bonds: that therein I may speak boldly, as I ought to speak.

CHAPTER 2

# MYSTERY DEFINED

Even Jesus disciples needed clarification. They had listened to the parables and they were not exactly sure of 2 things. Why Jesus used the parables as a primary way of teaching the crowds (Mt 13:10).

What the parables of the soils meant Luke 8-9. There are times when we hear the word of God and we are not fully comprehending either, why something is being taught the way it is or what exactly the teaching means. These questions are one's that we should be taking to the Lord, asking him that he might illuminate our understanding so we can clearly see what he is saying. The problem is not the clarity of Christ teaching, the problem is our understanding. Sometimes as with the disciples here our understanding has not been developed enough. We may be open and responsive as they were, but needing to grow and developed. While the lord is kind and patient with us, he delights in delivering us from slowness of hearth Luke 24:25.

**It's a Dual Purpose of Parables.**

To instruct and enlighten the open hearted. To those who have ears to hear they find that they have the ability to perceive that parables. Illustrate a spiritual truth and embrace them. This ability to understand the parables for what they really mean is a gift from God. Yet, it is not only the ability to know that the disciples received. They also received further teaching an explanation of the parables.

Jesus tells them that they had been given the secrets of the Kingdom of Heaven. What is this secret? When the New Testaments speaks of a Mystery of a Secret it does not mean that some impossible to understand teaching is being given or that a truth too high to grasp is being uttered. Rather it means that something that had been a mystery up until that point is now about to be clearly revealed and explained.

The Spirit tells us what this secret is in the following; The truth, now given to men by revelation in the person and mission of Jesus is that the kingdom which is to come finally in apocalyptic power as foreseen by Daniel has in fact entered the world in advance in hidden form to work secretly within and among men.

## To Conceal and Harden

Those who had continually received the word of God through the prophets and finally through the son of God and continually rejected it, God in his wisdom would no longer give explicit teaching but would use parables as a way to obscure or hide the truth as a means of judgment upon them.

Whatever prophecy has been declared, it will come in a parable. In other words, whatever God has spoken about in a person, place or thing it is revealed by a parable for the believer and to conceal the knowledge of the kingdom of God to the unbelievers.

CHAPTER 3

# MYSTERY OF THE LAWLESS ONE AND REBELLION THE FALLING AWAY

Paul uses the word mystery in 2 Thessalonians 2:
This chapter refers to the appearance of the Anti-Christ, the lawless one, the man of sin.

The phase "the day of the Lord" refers to a time of wrath and judgment by God.

An Apostle Paul Cities prerequisite that must be met before the day of the Lord begins. These two signs particularly the sign which will precede this judgment. The first is described as falling away-rebellion, the second as the rise of a renowned figure. Paul calls this figure a mystery and Jesus said it is given to you to know the mystery.

It may seem unfair that the disciples receive the mystery where the others don't but the parable of the sower explains why they have access to more information. They are the "good" soil that readily accepts the seed and nurtures it to germination yielding

30 fold, 60 fold and a 100 fold. They want to understand many things about the mysteries of the kingdom of God.

Paul explains the mystery of the rebellion and the Anti-Christ in 2 Thessalonians Chapter 2 verse 3 and 7.

Verse 3: "Let no man deceive you by any means: for *that day shall not come*, except there come a falling away first, and that man of sin be revealed, the son of perdition."

Verse 7: "For the mystery of lawlessness is already at work; only he who now restrains will do so until he is taken out of the way."

The word 'mystery' in the bible, is not talking about some mystifying or something that is to puzzling and hard to understand. A mystery in scripture is a truth that has been hidden from previous generations and is only made known to the people of God, by direct, divine revelation, and at God's appointed time.

In the New Testament mysteries that were hidden from Old Testament saints was truths that were to be revealed to the people of God, through Paul and by other New Testament writers during the Dispensation of the Grace of God the Church age.

Paul teaching of the many mysteries including; *"The Mystery of the "Falling Away"* (rebellion), *"The Mystery of the Man of Sin (The Lawless One) the Anti-Christ"*, *"The Mystery of Christ and the Church"*, *"The Mystery of the Gospel"*, *"The Mystery of Godliness"*, *"The Mystery of the Kingdom"*, and *"The Mystery of Christ in you the hope of glory."*

## In Thessalonians Chapter 2

The mystery of the lawlessness, for the mystery of lawlessness is already at work; only he who now restrains will do so until He is taken out of the way," then in verse "8" And then the lawless one will be revealed.

In these two scriptures the word is telling us that the lawless one comes after a mystery of the lawlessness. So the mystery of lawlessness is a forerunner of the lawless one because we know that a "Mystery is a parable and a Parable is a mystery."

The mystery of lawlessness was already well established in the days of Paul, and lawlessness continues to work its vetum/virus into the fabric of today's society. Even though it is largely hidden to the status of governments, nations, communities, and individuals under a veiled of spiritual blindness, and shrouded immorality. It is lurking in broken legal systems and biased political and justice department, and it lip-service to a form of godliness that is absent of truth of scripture and the fruit of righteousness.

Down through the centuries, anarchy, rebellion, and lawless behavior has been working to destroy every individual, society, nation and culture but God in his grace has always restricted the level of evil in the world through the dispensation of the Holy Spirit, who indwells all church-age Christians is restraining evil who are called to be the salt and light in a darken world. And now as we discern the signs of the times, the apostasy, the lawlessness and corruption like never before the tribulation is upon the world at this time and then the great tribulation which will have the rise of the lawless one, the Anti-Christ.

Today, there is a parable of the lawlessness that is accumulating from the deeds of a lawless one. If you have eyes to see and ears to hear you would know who it is! But if not, it is revealed in Chapter 9.

# CHAPTER 4

# PARABLES, SIGN OF THE TIMES

Jesus honors their heart by granting them their wishes. They stand in contrast to the Pharisees and Herodians who seek to destroy Jesus (Mk 3:6), the Crowd who wants to use him (Mk 3:7-10), and Jesus brothers who wish to hide him (Mk 3:21-31).

Jesus reveals this through his word in Matthew Chapter 16, how a parable is received.

1. The Pharisees also with the Sadducees came and tempting desired him that he would show them a sign from heaven.
2. He answered and said unto them, when it is evening, ye say it will be fair weather for the sky is red.
3. And in the morning, it will be foul weather today for the sky is red and lowering. O ye hypocrites, ye can discern the face of the sky; but can ye not discern the signs of the times?
4. A wicked and adulterous generation seeketh after a sign: And there shall no sign be given unto it, but the sign of the prophet Jonah.

Let's start with the word "sign." Sign means something that indicates a fact, conveys information, an act or event that reveals Divine knowledge. The Pharisees could discern the face of the sky or natural things but hey could not discern the sign of the times, the spiritual things. What these acts, people or event mean according to the spirit (word of God). Remember, these signs are call mysteries by Jesus Christ and Apostle Paul. The Pharisees could not see the signs of the times because they had rejected Christ.

Even though Jonah disobedience cause the storm and got him cast into the sea, God uses this event to reveal his 3 days and night in the belly of the earth. This was a parable for Christ to reveal the mystery in this life, the resurrection of the son of God. That he would be in the belly of the earth 3 days and nights.

5. And when his disciples were come to the other side, they had forgotten to take bread.
6. Then Jesus said unto them. Take heed and beware of the leaven of the Pharisees and of Sadducees.
7. And they reasoned among themselves, saying it is because we have taken no bread.
8. Which when Jesus perceived he said unto them, O ye of little faith, why reason ye among yourselves, because ye have brought no bread? Do ye not yet understand, neither remembers the five loaves of the five thousand, and how many baskets ye took up?
9. How is it that ye do not understand that I spake it not to you concerning bread, that ye should beware of the leaven of the Pharisees and of the Sadducees?
10. Then understood they how that he bade them now beware of the leaven of bread, but of the doctrine of the Pharisees and of the Sadducees? Jesus here uses the leaven as a parable to reveal the false teaching of the Pharisees, sad.
11. When Jesus came into the coasts of Caesar a Philippi he asked his disciples saying "whom do men say that I the son of man am?"

12. And they said, some say that thou art John the Baptist: some Elias: and others, Jeremias, or one of the Prophets.
13. He saith unto them, But whom say ye that I am?
14. And Simon Peter answered and said, Thou art the Christ, the son of the living God.
15. And Jesus answered and said unto him, "Blessed art thou, Simon Bar jona: For flesh and blood hath not revealed it unto thee, but my father which is in heaven. In verse 13-17 Jesus is teaching how man could not know (perceive) God or spiritual things only God the Father knows the things of God. This is what we have been teaching in cor. 2 2 and Mark 4 and now in Mt. Ch 16. Like the word says in Eph. 4:4-9, 11-12

| | |
|---|---|
| Verse 4: | There is a one body and one spirit, just as you were called in one hope of your calling. |
| Verse 5: | One Lord, One Faith, One Baptism. |
| Verse 6: | One God and Father of all, who is above all, and through all and in you all. |
| Verse 7: | But to each one of us, grace was given according to the measure of Christ's gift. |
| Verse 11: | And he himself gave some to be apostles, some prophets, some evangelists and some pastors and teachers. |
| Verse 12: | For the equipping of the saints for the work of ministry for the edifying of the body of Christ. The Church in Mt. 16:18 that he would build on the rock, Peter the Apostle. |

## Matthew 16: Verse 18-19

Verse 18:   And I say also unto thee, that thou art Peter and upon this rock I will build my Church; and the gates of hell shall not prevail against it.

Verse 19:   And I will give unto thee the keys of the kingdom of heaven and whatsoever thou shalt bind on earth shall be bound in heaven: and whatsoever thou shall loose on earth shall be loosed in heaven.

Verse 19:   is telling the church that Jesus has given spiritual authority to illustrate heavenly power. He has given us earthly, Power to reflect heavenly authority.

# CHAPTER 5

# COMPARING SPIRITUAL THINGS TO SPIRITUAL THINGS

The kingdom of God does not just mean going to church, although that is part of it. It means any situation on heaven or earth that reflects Gods power, sovereignty, and holiness. Jesus is willing to give the "12" and the other disciple's special understanding of how God is working at that moment, to fulfill his will in the earth with a parable of Christ to reveal the kingdom of heaven in this life. To you it is given to know the mysteries.

Another word for mystery is "secret" is from the Greek root word mysterion, from which we get "mystery" it refers to something hidden, and not readily available to the public. It is only discovered and understood through divine revelation in this case Jesus providing an explanation, see Mk 4:12-34. Daniel and Joseph experienced the mystery when they interpreted prophetic dreams.

Nebuchadnezzar and Pharaoh's dreams couldn't be interpreted through stars or a standard book of symbolism, Dan 2:18 and Gen

41:1 only understood dreams because God revealed what they meant. In our case, the secrets are revealed through the Bible which is a recording of several vision, parable and revelation along with the Holy Spirit.

Jesus says that the crowd receives everything in parables. This includes Jesus actions as well as his verbal teaching even Jesus physical miracles have a deeper meaning than what's seen on the surface. You can't be what you can't see!

Importantly, there is a difference between human wisdom and the secret, hidden wisdom of God. God's wisdom includes his plan, established before the world was formed, to offer righteousness and salvation to those who believe in Christ's death on the cross as the payment for their own sin.

Human wisdom is based on what can be observed with the senses and worked out with human reason. That wisdom simply cannot see or understand the truth of God. In order to believe God's wisdom, he must reveal it to us through his own spirit. As our spirit knows our thoughts, God's spirit knows his thoughts and helps us to believe his revelation of those thoughts to us. The spirit of the world is limited to understanding and believing in only what can he observed with the senses. Christians have been given the spirit of God. For each person who comes to God through faith in Christ. Paul's work was to use human words but not bare human wisdom to help interpret the spiritual truths revealed to those who believe so that they could understand them more fully. The Holy Spirit revealed this through Paul in I Corinthians Chapter 2.

Verse 1: And so it was me, brothers and sisters. When I came to you, I did not come with eloquence or human wisdom as I proclaimed to you the testimony about God.

Verse 2: For I resolved to know nothing while I was with you except Jesus Christ and him crucified.

Verse 3: I came to you in weakness with great fear and trembling.

Verse 4: My message and my preaching were not with wise and persuasive words, but with a demonstration of the Spirit's power.

Verse 5: So that your faith might not rest on human wisdom, but on God's power.

Verse 6: We do, however, speak a message of wisdom among the mature, but not the wisdom of this age or of the rulers of this age, who are coming to nothing.

Verse 7: No, we declare God's wisdom, a mystery that has been hidden and that God destined for our glory before time began.

Verse 8: None of the rulers of this age understood it, for if they had, they would not have crucified the Lord of glory.

Verse 9: However, as it is written:

"What no eye has seen, what no ear has heard, and what no human mind has conceived" the things God has prepared for those who love him.

Verse 10: These are the things God has revealed to us by his Spirit. The Spirit searches all things, of God.

Verse 11: For who knows a person's thoughts except their own spirit within them? In the same way no one knows the thoughts of God except the Spirit of God.

Verse 12: What we have received is not the spirit of the world, but the Spirit who is from God, so that we may understand what God has freely given us.

Verse 13: This is what we speak, not in words taught us by human wisdom but in words taught by the Spirit, explaining spiritual realities with Spirit-taught words.

Verse 14: The person without the Spirit does not accept the things that come from the Spirit of God but considers them foolishness, and cannot understand them because they are discerned only through the Spirit.

Verse 15: The person with the Spirit makes judgments about all things, but such a person is not subject to merely human judgment.

Verse 16: For "Who has known the mind of the Lord so as to instruct him?" But we have the mind of Christ. Amen!

How wonderful this word is to know that we have the mind of Christ to compare spiritual things to spiritual things. Verse 13.

All of Jesus ministry is hidden from those who reject him. This doesn't make God's truth hidden or mystical or even complicated, it just requires that a person care enough and willing to accept Jesus Christ as Lord and savior. The biggest parable of all may be that he did not come to save the Jews from the Romans, but to save everyone from sin and death.

Remember it was sin that cause man to become spiritually blind. It was sin that got Adam and Eve cast out of the garden.

St. John 3:3 "Except you be born again, you cannot see the kingdom of heaven. Now it's not talking about "By and By" in the sky" when you go to heaven. But you must be born again from above.

Verse 5: Except he be born of the water and of the spirit, he cannot enter the kingdom of heaven.

Jesus explain seeing the kingdom in Verse 3 and entering heaven in Verse 5.

You cannot have, what you cannot see by faith. We walk by faith, not by sight.

PARABLES

## The Parable of the Kingdom of Heaven on Earth

Number 13: 1-2
And the Lord spake unto Moses, saying.

Verse 2: Send thou men, that they may search the land of Canaan, which I give unto the children of Israel: of every tribe of their fathers shall ye send a man everyone a ruler among them.

Verse 27: And they told him, and said we came unto the land whither thou sentest us and surely it floweth with milk and honey and this the fruit of it.

Verse 28: Nevertheless the people be strong that dwell in the land, and the cities and walled, and very great and moreover we saw the children of Anak there.

Verse 30: And Caleb stilled the people before Moses, and said, let us go up at once, and possess it for we are well able to overcome it.

Verse 31: But the men that went up with him said, we be not able to go up against the people, for they are stronger than we.

Verse 32: And they brought up an evil report of the land which they had searched unto the children if Israel, saying, The land through which we have gone to search it, is a land that eateth up the inhabitants thereof: and all the people that we saw in it are men of a great statue.

Verse 33: And there we saw the giants, the sons of Anak, which come of the giants: and we were in our own sight as grasshoppers, and so we were in their sight.

Chapter 13: 1 And all the congregation lifted up their voice, and cried and the people wept that night.

The children murmured against Moses and Aaron.

Verse 26: And the Lord spake unto Moses and Aaron saying.

Verse 27: How long shall I bear with this evil congregation, which murmur against me? I have heard the murmurings of the children of Israel, which they murmur against me.

Verse 29: Your carcases shall fall in this wilderness and all that were mumbered of you, according to your whole number, from 20 years old and upward, which have murmured against me.

Verse 30: Doubtless ye shall not come into the land, concerning which I sware to make you dwell therein, save Caleb the son of Jephunneh and Joshua the son of Nun.

The promise land is a parable for heaven on earth. A land flowing with milk and honey.

In Heb. 25:2  The land shall keep the Sabbath day. This was a parable for Christ, to reveal his kingdom on earth in this life.
They did not except the word, so they could not enter the kingdom. You may ask yourself how does this apply to me?

In John 3:3  Jesus answered and said unto him, verily, verily, I say unto thee, except a man be born again, he cannot see the kingdom of God.

This scripture is referring to the kingdom of God on the earth, now!

St. John 3:5  Verily, verily I say unto thee, except a man be born of water and of the spirit, he cannot enter into the kingdom of God. This is referring to being with God in eternal life. Therefore Roman 10:9, That if you confess with your mouth the Lord Jesus and believe in your heart that God has raised him from the dead, you will be saved. Jesus is our promise land today Heb. 25:2. Mt. 12:8

It's God Word that framed The beginning to be a (parable) in the end.

That why the word says in Is. 46:10

"I declared the end from ancient times the things that are not yet done. My counsel shall stand, and I will do all my pleasure.

Eccl. 1:9  That which has been is what will be, that which is done is what will be done and there is nothing new under the sun.

Rev. 1:8  I am the Alpha and the Omega, the beginning and the end, says the Lord, who is and who was and who is to come, the Almighty.

# CHAPTER 6

# ENOCH, PARABLE OF THE ELECT

Enoch saw Jesus, the Holy one in the beginning, and showed him the end. Enoch was a parable for Christ, to reveal that which is to come in this life! Enoch was referred more than a lot of other servants of God to name a few, all the minor prophets, more than Ezekiel, Jeremiah but yet we never talk about him. Why is that? Is there something about Enoch or the other books that you have not seen.

**Let's look at a few scripture to document this truth.**

In Genesis, the writer Moses

Chapter 5:24     "And Enoch walked with God, and he was not for God took him. In Hebrews, the writer Paul the Apostle

Chapter 11:5     "By faith Enoch was taken away so that he did not see death, and was not found because God had taken him. For before he was taken he had this testimony, that he pleased God.

In Jude, ____ the Apostle Jude.
Chapter 1:14   "Now Enoch, the seventh from Adam, prophesied about these men also, saying," "Behold the Lord comes with ten thousands of his Saints."

## Let's look at Enoch writing

### Enoch Chapter 1

1. The words of the blessing of Enoch, wherewith he blessed the Elect and righteous, who will be.
2. Living in the day of tribulation, when all the wicked and godless are to be removed. And he took up his parable and said Enoch a righteous man, whose eyes were opened by God, saw the vision of the Holy one in heaven, which the angels showed me, and from them I heard everything, and from them I understood as I saw, but not for this generation, but for to come. Concerning the elect I said, and took up my parable concerning them: The Holy Great one will come forth his dwelling.
7. And the earth shall be wholly, rent in sunder, and all that is upon the earth shall perish, and there shall be a judgment upon all men.
8. But with the righteous he will make peace and will protect the elect, and mercy shall be upon them. And they shall belong to God, and they shall be prospered, and they shall all be blessed. And he will help them all, and light shall appear unto them and he will make peace with them.
9. And behold! He cometh with ten thousands of his Holy Ones to execute judgment upon all and to destroy all the ungodly.

## Let look at Enoch through the scriptures.

Enoch the first man to be taken by God and did not see death. He is of the antedilavan period in the Hebrew Bible. Enoch was the son of Jared and fathered Methuselah. This Enoch known as the Ethiopian Prophet, The Lost Prophet of the Bible. Greater than Abraham holier than Moses. Is not to be confused with Cain's son Enoch Gen. 4:17. The text of the book of Gen. 5:7, Enoch lived 365 years befored he was taked.

Why were books left out of the bible? These books have only been known to few people, might have been left out because their content does not fit well into that of other books. Some of the Apocrypha were written at a later date, and were therefore not included or is this a case of deliberate sabotage by the enemy of the truth. Remember the prince of darkness do not want the light to shine on you. It is lack of knowledge that causes destruction/

The dead sea scrolls include over 225 copies of biblical books that date up to 1,200 years earlier so I ask question. What is it that you don't know?

| | |
|---|---|
| Hosea 4:6 | My people are destroyed for lack of knowledge because thou hast rejected knowledge, I will also reject thee, that thou shall be no priest to me: seeing thou hast forgotten the law of the God, I will also forgot thy children. |
| And in 2 Pt 1:2 | Grace and peace be multiplied through the knowledge of our Lord Jesus Christ. |

Let me testify to the power of the knowledge of him who has a call us to glory and virtue. I had to go 3 thousand miles to Tacoma, WA. And in the house that I was staying, the previous owner of that house left a Original King James version from the 1800's. And in that bible were several books that are not in the New King James version. To name a few 1,2 Macabees, The history of Suzanna. But it was the book of Enoch where I saw the "Parable" and the rest is history. Now when you take all the books that are not in your bible, you have to ask the question what do I not know? Remember faith cometh by hearing and hearing the word of God. Rom. 10:17

# CHAPTER 7

# ELECTED TO BE PERFECTED

In Roman Chapter 8

These scriptures in Romans Chapter 8 reveal how the new covenant is in the old covenant and the old covenant is in the new covenant overt.

Roman 8 express method describing the qualities, principles and character of the elect. It sound just like what parable Enoch was proclaiming in the Genesis, The Beginning.

| | |
|---|---|
| Romans Verse:28 | And we know that all things work together for good to those who love God, to those who are the called according to his purpose. |
| Verse 29: | For whom he foreknew, he also predestined to be conformed to the image of his son, that he might be firstborn among many brethren. |
| Verse 30: | Moreover whom he predestined, these he also called: whom he called: these he also justified: and whom he justified these he also glorified. |

Verse 31: What then shall we say to these things? If God is for us, who can be against us?

Verse 32: He who did not spare his own son, but delivered him up for us all, how shall he not with him also freely give us all things?

Verse 33: Who shall bring a charge against God's elect? It is God who justifies.

Verse 34: Who is he who condemns? It is Christ who died, and furthermore is also risen. Who is even at the right hand of God who also makes intercession for us.

Verse 35: Who shall separate us from the love of Christ? Shall tribulation, or distress, persecution, or famine, or nakedness, or peril, or sword?

Verse 36: As it is written:"For your sake we are killed all day long: we are accounted as sheep for the slaughter."

Verse 37: Yet in all these things we are more than conquerors through him who loved us.

Verse 38: For I am persuaded that neither death nor life, nor angels nor principalities nor powers, nor kings present nor things to come.

Verse 39: Nor heights nor depth, nor any other created thing, shall be able to separate us from the love of God which is in Christ Jesus our Lord. Hallelujah!

Romans Chapter 12 are perfect in that they all described the elect in the image and character of the parables for Jesus Christ in the end-times which we are now in according the parable of the Fig tree.

CHAPTER 8

# THE PARABLE OF THE WEDDING FEAST

This is what the kingdom will be like in the end. The wedding feast has great significant in the Bible. It is the day when God will gather all his redeemed and they will enjoy his presence in complete love and glory.

By the King's order, banquet invitations go out. The King's servants sent to call those who were invited to the wedding feast but they would not come. Mt. 22:3. They offer a host of excuses and mistreat the servants, so the king punishes them. Mt. 22:5-7. The King now dispatches his servants; Go therefore to the main roads and invite to the wedding feast as many as you find Mt. 22:9

Jesus is describing the offer of the gospel first to the Jews and then to the Gentiles. The Jewish nation had decisively rejected the offer God made to them through his prophets. For that rejection, Jesus announces the judgment God will bring the Roman armies destruction of Jerusalem in 70 AD. But in that rejection is the occasion of the gospel being extent to the Gentiles. The result is that the wedding hall filled with guests Mt. 22:10.

But then something unexpected happens. The King joins his guest and discovers a man who had no wedding garment. The man can give no reason why has no garment in an act of eschatological judgment, the king order his attender to bind the man hands and feet and cast him into the outer darkness. In that place there will be weeping and gnashing of teeth. Jesus ends his story by pronouncing the aphorism that summarizes the parables meaning for many are called, but few are chosen.

## The Called

What does Jesus mean by, For many are called, but few are chosen? To answer, we must understand what means here by call and choose. The call runs through the parable. In the Greek text, the servant are said to call those who had been called to the feast Mt. 22:3. The Jewish invites are the "called ones" Mt. 22:4,8. The Servants are then commanded to "call" the Gentiles 22:9. The Word translated called in verse 14 belongs to the same word family as that translated called in verses 3, 4, 8 and 9.

This pattern helps us understand the nature of the call in this parable. It is the summons or invitation of God through his servants, prophets in the Old Testament, minister in the New. This call bids hearers to repent and believe the good news the servants proclaim. It is possible to refuse as many Jews did. Jesus teaches that those who refuses the call are culpable for refusing it.

But it is also possible to respond to this call in a non saving way. The man without the wedding garment in 22:12 presumably responded to the invitation. But his lack of the garment proves he doesn't belong at the feast, and he is justly banished. What is the wedding garment? It likely pictures the first of salvation freely offered to the gospel. Only those who receive this gift will be seated at the wedding banquet of the Lamb at the consummation of all things.

## The Chosen

Who are they who sincerely respond to the call and receive Christ in faith? Jesus calls them the "Chosen" or as the Greek word maybe translated the elect (Eph. 1:4). Only these chosen ones will constitute the company of the redeemed when Christ returns in glory. God's eternal choice ensures they will respond sincerely to the call.

Since the New Testament elsewhere joins calling with election (see Tim 1:9, Rom 8:30). What does Jesus mean when he says there are some who are called but not chosen?

"The external call goes to all people. But only the elect experience the internal call."

The answer lies in a distinction necessary to understand the way the biblical writes speaks of call in this parable, Jesus speaks of call in an external sense. It is the summons of God through the gospel message. This call bids men and women to come to Christ by way of repentance and faith.

In other places the biblical writers speak of call in an internal sense. For instance, Paul speaks of this internal call in Icor. 1:24, this is the effective saving work of the spirit of Christ in conjunction with the gospels outward call.

This internal call powerfully and effectively turns the sinner from his sin to Jesus Christ. The external call goes to all people. But only the elect will in God's time experience the internal call. For them the gospel is indeed the power of God unto salvation, Rom 1:16.

What are the lessons Jesus teaches us in this parable? First to refuse the summons of God through his messengers, God will hold those who refuse that summon responsible on judgment day. Second, Jesus wants us to realize there is a more subtle way to refuse the summons. One may pay lip service to the external call but never truly embrace Jesus as offered in that call. Even this refusal subjects us to God's just judgment.

The bad news is we have no power in ourselves to change our rebellious hearts. The good news is God is pleased to change rebellious hearts by the invincible power of his spirit. If we have responded to the external call in repentance and faith, it is only because God has first been at work in us to turn us to himself in Christ salvation is truly by grace alone. This truth is unsettling. He wants us to find salvation and life in him alone by grace alone. And only in Christ may we find an everlasting, unshakeable foundation.

# CHAPTER 9

# THE PARABLE OF THE REBELLION

**Verse 35 Tribulation**

Because Christ has redeemed us from the curse of the law (sin and death) from which the tribulation is the fruit of Mt. 24:21, during these end times the elect will be more than conquerors in all these things.

The abomination of desolation that Jesus prophesied about in Mt. 24:15.

Jesus tells us that it was spoken by Daniel the Prophet, which makes it a parable, a parable of Anti-Christ, to reveal the man of sin in this life. Daniel original prophecy Dan.12:11, 9:27 has several fulfillment.

In 168 BC when his army, Syrian King Antiochus Espihanes erected an altar to the Greek God Zeus on the temple mount in Jerusalem and offered swine upon it, Maccabean Ch. 1:44-61

This intensified the Jewish resistance leading to the Maccabean revolt once the Jews retook Jerusalem, they cleansed and rededicated the temple in 165 BC an act commemorated in the Jewish Hanukah celebration.

In 63 BC, the Roman General Pompey desecrated the temple by entering the Holy of Holies, finding it empty. He did not plunder the temple furnishing or treasury.

The first temple was built in 1000 B.C. by King Solomon after David conquered Jerusalem capital, it was destroyed in 586 B.C. by Nebuchadnezzar, King of Babylon. What Jesus spoke of in Mt. 24:2 is the desecration of the temple and the destruction of Jerusalem by the Romans armies in 70 A.D. after the Jews rebelled. The Temple was completely destroyed by the Roman legions, and not one stone was left on another as Jesus declared Verse 2.

However another fulfillment awaits, a short time before Christ returns, armies will once again surround Jerusalem and an abomination will appear in the City. As Mt. 24:21 says this act inaugurates the time of Great Tribulation.

What form this end time abomination will take is not specifically mentioned, but it will likely be some action taken by the invading army led by a satanic figure or an idol erected in the temple precincts as in the former desolations. (In the Old Testament abomination is synonymous with idol). It could also be something as simple as the army brutal destruction of the temple mount and its buildings. The abomination of desolation is one of the Chief signs of the end time that Christian is command to watch Mt.24:42. Jesus tells us to watch the picture (parables) that he has reveal to his saints. God has always kept his chosen people inform weather the blessing for obedience are the cursing for disobedience revealed through the parables. It's not a coincidence that Trump impeachment, indictment insurrection and Covid-19 arrived at the same time on the scene.

But a divine consequences, the event that we witness on January 6, 2021. The insurrection of the capitol temple was a parable of the abomination desolation.

The main figure in the world system doing the tribulation will be the Anti-Christ and false prophet. This is another way of judgment coming on those who reject Jesus, 2 Thessalonians Ch. 2:10-12.

Jude 1:11, refers to the Old Testament false teacher. Parables for false prophets Jude bring three indictments against the false teachers 1: They were following cains example 2: like Balaam they had chosen profit above integrity and 3: like Korah, they had rebelled against God.

Jude condemns the false teachers by pronouncing, woe to them! He anticipates the terrible fate of the false teachers under God's judgment. The prophet Isaiah also pronounced woe upon those who, had turned away from the Lord and his truth. He declared, "Woe to those who call evil good and good evil, who put darkness for light and light for darkness, who put bitter for sweet and sweet for bitter!" Woe to those who are wise in their own eyes and shrewd in their own sight Is. 5:20-21.

The mystery of the rebellion and the lawlessness is in full effect, if you have eyes to see and can perceive and ears to hear and can understand what Paul; mean when he says in 2 Thessalonians 2:7. For the mystery of lawlessness is already at work. Let the Holy Spirit show you a parable to them that have eyes to see and perceive.

## THE PARABLE OF THE LAWLESS ONE

# THE WAYS AND ACTS OF A FALSE PROPHET

What they did.

Balaam.
Gave evil counsel
To Israel. Known
As false prophet

Trump
Gave evil Council
On Coronavirus
Said it was a hoax.
Known as a liar.

Antiochus.
Army March to
Temple erected
Greek god zeus

Trump
Jun 1 March to'
Temple an,
Erected a prop
Holding Bible.

Nebuchadnezzar
Made decree to'
Worship image.

I have built the
Kingdom by my
Power.

Trump
Made a policy to
Stop immigrants
Crossing border.
I alone can make
America great.

Sun myung moon.
Claim to be
The Messiah.

Trump
Said he was the
Chosen One.

Jim Jones
Gave Council to
Drink poison.

Trump
Gave Council to
Associates to
Drink the poison
Of corruption.
Gave Council on
Hatred, racism
And Violence

What it cause

Brought a plague
That killed 24,000.

Tens of thousands
More are dying
Than should be.
U.S. shutdown
Loss of jobs

Desecrated the
Temple mt.
Intensified resistance
Leading to Macc. Revolt.

Violated the sanctity
Of Temple intensified
Protesters and
Military outcry

Cast three boys into
Fiery furnace and
Daniel in loin
Cage. They would
Not worship image.

Cast children into
Cages.
Made America into
Chaos and disorder
At the brink of
Collapse

Cult like behavior

Cult like behavior

More than 900
Was killed

They were
Convicted and Sent
To Prison+

America has a racism epedemic

---

Here's what the word of God says about these characteristics Hosea chapter 10 verse 13.

You have plowed wickedness, you have reaped iniquity, you have eaten the fruit of Lies because you have trusted in your multitude of your Mighty Men.

# TRUMP, A FALSE PROPHET FOR FINANCIAL PROFIT *(PAGE 54)*

All Prophets are not just a spokesperson for a religious entity but can be any leader or representative figure in society. To choose financial wealth over spiritual health is rebellion and produces the curse of disease, sickness and death. The coronavirus is not just a pandemic but a Divine judgment that is prophetic.

There is now new thing under the sun that which is to be has already been done. God declared the end from the beginning and from ancient times, so his elect can know the signs. But to the others, they have eyes to see, but they do not perceive; they have ears to hear, but they do not understand the parables for Christ, to reveal mystery of the kingdom of God in this life.

During the ancient days of Israel, there was a prophet named Balaam that seduced Israel, and the plagues killed 24,000 of them. President Trump is like the false prophet Balaam and nothing like the righteous kind of Salem. Balaam seduced Israel into sexual adultery; Trump seduces the evangelical into apostasy. Trump and Balaam love the wealth of unrighteous gain and that goes without shame.

All witches are not old, ugly women riding a broom, but can be and old man bewitching the people with lies, and he's a spirit of gloom and doom. God made everything to himself, even the wicked for the day of evil. The president took the oath of office to be the Commander and Chief but operates like Baghdad the thief. He's nothing lie King Cyrus; he is corrupt like the Coronavirus. The coronavirus like leprosy symbolizes the corruption which is sin, and results in the separation of the community of men (social distancing). It is a sign of sin that is a vivid and a graphic picture. A spiritual defilement that is unclean, ugly, and painful in nature.

Everything became corrupt that he touches, and the evidence is more than a hunch. He was world renown as Balaam was for hire as a driver and a prophet; they are both for financial profit. All these talk about the President's celebrity, why he treats anyone who disagrees with him perversity. President Trump's culture reflects chaos, disorder, and confusion. He is encouraging the breakdown of the Constitution to stay in office with a strong delusion. Glorifying the use of lies, belittle, and slander with a text . . . false prophet, what are you going to produce next?

The administration represents the psychotic soul; they are cultivating the evils of old. The President and his congregation or administration has compromised with the doctrine of Balaam error. And now America is in terror! America, America, how you have failed. You have forsaken the Constitution and Bible doctrine and cannot prevail because your materialism has outdistanced your moralism. And your civilization has outdistanced your spiritualization.

There must be a culture in a nation that reflects the righteousness spiritually. We have to learn from history, or we are going to end in misery. A false prophet tells thousands of lies, and it will produce an immoral nation to its demise. This is the sign of the false prophet in our times.

The Balaam story told by John in Revelation (Chapter 2 Verse 14) is a strange and mysterious but true story written in the word of God in Numbers: 22-25. The Israelites were camped in Moab following Moses. The Midianites and the Moabites were receiving oracles from God through Balaam. One of those many prophets, who God had dispensed throughout the world since the dawn of history.

PARABLES

Balaam was a Mesopotamian. He was, therefore, a foreigner among the Moabites and the Amorites. He was considered a soothsayer and diviner of considerable power. The intrusion of the Israelites alarmed Balak, King of Moab. He called upon the service of the prophet Balaam who had a reputation for powerful divining. Balak wanted Balaam to put a curse upon the Israelites so as to stop their progress in Moab.

Balaam did both right and wrong. He refused to make any pronouncement other than what God said. Even though the king pressed Balaam for another message, Balaam would give him nothing but God's. The king wanted a curse to put on the Israelites, but Balaam gave them a blessing. Time and again the leader of Moab asks Balaam to have another go at divining the message they wanted. Each time the Lord gave Balaam a stronger version of the truth and told him to pronounce a blessing instead of a curse. Balaam repeated the blessings, faithfully defying the king. His attitude was "I must be careful to speak what the Lord put in my mouth." (Numbers 23:12).

False prophet Balaam was too easy led away from God's truth into error, and he in turn led many others astray (see Numbers 31:8, 16; and Revelation 2:14). Instead of giving the Council of God, he taught people to practice idolatry and to commit fornication. It was his council that caused the children of Israel to sin and to suffer a terrible plague (Numbers 25:1-9 and 31:14-16). He loved money more than the truth. For all Balaam talked about speaking only what God put into his mouth, he was wishing to curse the children of Israel for the generous fee Balaam would pay him. Instead of loving righteousness, Balaam loved the way of unrighteous gain (2 Peter 2:15-16).

Balaam and Unfaithful Prophet.

By the power granted him by God, Balaam had the opportunity to demonstrate the power of the true God against the deception of false gods and idols. When Balaam pronounced a blessing or a curse, it worked. Balak said as much as when he summoned Balaam to curse the Israelites (Numbers 22:6).

Sure, Balaam ordered a blessing instead of a curse. What would be the point in Balaam pronouncing a curse if God was going to give a blessing? Balaam would look stupid and damage his reputation. However, Balaam kept going along with Balak's repeated attempts to get a curse from God upon the Israelites because, like Balak, he hoped the situation might change.

Even though Balaam was right to speak only what God told him to speak, Balaam gets very bad criticism repeatedly in the Bible. God was angry with Balaam because he went to Balak (Numbers 23:3). Balaam had wanted to curse the children of Israel, to be paid for hire (Deuteronomy 23:3-6). Balaam was killed by the Israelites in the days of Joshua (Joshua 13:22). The prophet Nehemiah recalled how the Moabites met not the children with bread and water but hired Balaam against them that he should curse them, albeit God turned the curse into a blessing (Nehemiah 13:2). Peter recalls how Balaam loved the wages of unrighteousness (2 Peter 2:15-16). Jude recalls how for pay the error Balaam was committed (Jude 1:11). And Jesus recalls how Balaam kept teaching Balak to put a stumbling block before the children of Israel, to eat things sacrificed to idols, and to commit sexual immortality (Revelation 2:14).

God commanded Balaam clearly, "Do not go with them. You should not curse the people, for they are blessed" (Numbers 22:12). God gave Balaam an unmistakable sign. The incident with the donkey and the angel left Balaam without any excuse for continuing to compromise with what Balak desired.

God judged Balaam worthy of death. The reason was that Balaam still insisted on going to Balak. But for his donkey, Balaam would have been killed by the angel of the Lord (Numbers 22:33). This was God's permissive will. God provided a savior for Balaam. Balaam's donkey was Balaam's suffering savior.

God sometimes speaks through unholy instruments. Just because God is using an individual or thing that does not mean they are walking with God. God was long-suffering to Balaam. God was showing patience with Balaam's pondering to Balak's three attempts to change God's word (Numbers 24:10-13). God punished Balaam's hears who had compromised with death. God killed those who heeded Balaam's wicked counseling (Numbers 25:1-8 and 31:14-18). God finally killed Balaam as he died at the hand of the Israelites (Joshua 13:22).

Doesn't Balaam's ways remind you of another leader in today's events? America's fruitlessness in spiritual health has produced the sin, corruption, disease, sickness and death. America has become barren and rotten. The coronavirus symbolizes the curse that was put on the fig tree by Jesus Christ which we are now seeing in the pandemic. From the very beginning in the Garden of Eden (Genesis 3:17-18), the Word says, "curse is the ground for thy sake, in sorrow shall thou eat of it all the days of their life. Thorns and thistles, shall it bring forth to thee." The word thorn refers to pain and suffering. "The Fig tree Parable"

## The curse of the fig tree and the coronavirus in America.

The fig tree event (Matthew 21:19) is a metaphor for Israel and America. It was President John Adams who said, "The general principles upon which the father's achieved independence were the general principles of the Bible doctrine." The national motto established by Congress in 1956 is "In God we trust" and "God bless America." These are the principles by which America was a blessed nation.

Throughout the Old Testament Israel is described as a vineyard, a tree or planting. Every Israelite knew the first fruits of the harvest belonged to God. They must yield spiritual fruit as his covenant people. Israel's fruitfulness, literal and otherwise, is not the basis of their relationship with God, but is God who gives fruitfulness (Deuteronomy 7:13). The lack of fruitfulness is a sign of God's curse/plague for their rebellion (Deuteronomy 11:17). So, two exiles, the Assyrian and Babylonian, God pours out the curse of barrenness, and Israel becomes a rotten and barren fig tree (Jeremiah 29:17).

Then Jesus moves his focus to the temple in Jerusalem where there is no fruit. The fig tree once again has failed, the Passover celebration, the God's house of prayer, and Jesus finds it a den of thieves. Lots of action, leaves, but no fruit. So, upon the fruitless tree Jesus pours out divine judgment again. The future pointing act of the cursing of the temple.

The fig tree cursing is not just about historical Israel; it is about the people of God throughout time, especially America. God expected his covenant people to have fruit that did not wither on the road between Bethany and Jerusalem. Christians by definition must produce spiritual fruit. It is one thing to lack fruit out of season. It is another thing to lack while pretending you have it.

Therefore, the coronavirus is here because of man's behavior, the consequences of sin. God said it in Hosea 10:13, "You have plowed wickedness you have reaped iniquity, you have eaten the fruit of lies, because you trusted in your own way, in the multitude of your mighty men. (also, Galatians 6:7-8), be not deceived, God is not mocked, whatsoever a man soweth, that so shall be reap. They that soweth to the flesh shall of the flesh reap corruption. And they that soweth to the Spirit everlasting life." America has reaped death and cases in the pandemic is no accident along with the highest incarceration rate, the highest drug abuse cases and gun violence, and homicide rate in the world. So, the coronavirus shutdown is the fruit of a spiritual breakdown! And is not just a pandemic but a divine judgment that is apocalyptic. Now you should be asking, "What is next?"

Barren and rotten judgments on Israel

The Assyrian captivity 732 bc

The Babylonian captivity for 70 years

Jesus curses the fig tree in Matthew 21 verse 11 on his way to the temple for being fruitless.

Jesus empties the temple of the money changes; he said you have made my house of prayer a den of Thieves.

Jerusalem and the temple were desolated by the Roman in 70 AD

70 years after the birth of Israel the branch of Israel, America was shut down December 2018 which was a prophetic Act of Judgment for America on this coronavirus shut down today which you are now living in.

Jesus said in Matthew CHAPTER 24 verse 32 learn the parable of the fig tree.

He was referring to his Vineyard the fig tree Israel.

# PARABLES

With the working (parable) of the lawless one in today's events let us know that the Anti-Christ is near even at the door. The Holy Spirit is not restraining the sin and the evil in the world. That's why there is so much violence, sickness and death.

He that has ears to hear, let him hear and he that has eyes to see let him see the mysteries of the kingdom of God. Remember what Jesus said in St. John Chapter 3 Verse 1, 2 and 3.

Verse 1: There was a man of the Pharisees named Nicodemus, a ruler of the Jews.

Verse 2: The same came to Jesus by night and said unto him, "Rabbi we know that you are a teacher who has come from God. For no man can do these miracles that thou doest, except God be with him.

This scripture show that Nicodemus does not see (perceive) that Jesus is the son of God in the flesh, so Jesus tell him why he cannot see the kingdom in verse 3.

Verse 3: Jesus Answered and said unto, verily, verily, I say unto thee, except a man be born again he cannot see the kingdom of God.

Verse 4: Nicodemus said unto him. How can a man be born when he is old? Can he enter the second time into his mother's womb and be born?

Verse 5: Jesus answered, verily, verily, I say unto thee except a man be born of water and of the Spirit, he cannot enter into the kingdom of God.

Verse 6: That which is born of the flesh is flesh and that which is born of Spirit is spirit.

Just like you were born of the water in the flesh to enter the natural world. You must be born of the water and of the Spirit to enter the kingdom of God, the spiritual world. So then unless you are born again you cannot see the kingdom of God in this world and you cannot enter the spiritual dominion later (time appointed).

So today, if you have not accepted Jesus Christ as your Lord and Savior, repent, confess your sins and believe that Jesus Christ is the son of the living God, the father of Glory which none of the rulers of this world knew, for had they known they would not have crucified the Lord of Glory. This is the wisdom we speak in a mystery, the hidden wisdom of God which he ordained before the ages for our glory.

Parables for Christ, to reveal the mystery of the knowledge of God in this life. The spiritual reality of the social and political culture that are happening in the world are done in parables.

**Grace Ministries**
Gifted Resources at Christian Excellence
By
Ruler Roberts Jr.

www.ingramcontent.com/pod-product-compliance
Lightning Source LLC
LaVergne TN
LVHW020438080526
838202LV00055B/5245